Moon Zoo

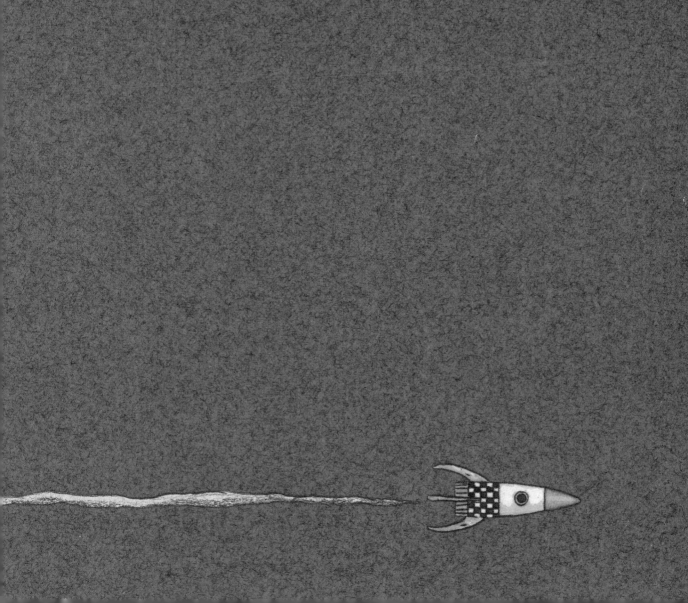

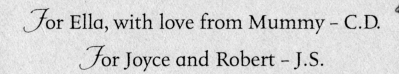

For Ella, with love from Mummy – C.D.

For Joyce and Robert – J.S.

First published 2004 by Macmillan Children's Books
This edition published 2009 by Macmillan Children's Books
a division of Macmillan Publishers Ltd
20 New Wharf Road, London N1 9RR
Basingstoke and Oxford
Associated companies throughout the world
www.panmacmillan.com

ISBN: 978-0-230-74805-7

Text copyright © Carol Ann Duffy 2004
Illustrations copyright © Joel Stewart 2004
Moral rights asserted

1 3 5 7 9 8 6 4 2

A CIP catalogue record for this book is available from the British Library.
Printed in Belgium by Proost

nesta

Carol Ann Duffy gratefully acknowledges a Fellowship from NESTA.
NESTA – the National Endowment for Science, Technology and the Arts –
was set up in 1998 to support innovation and creative potential in the UK.

Moon Zoo

Written by
Carol Ann Duffy

Illustrated by
Joel Stewart

MACMILLAN
CHILDREN'S BOOKS

At the foot of the mountains of the moon

Is a lunar zoo.

It has ten baboons.

They jump twenty feet into outer space

And flash their bottoms at the human race!

In a crater of the moon squats a huge gorilla –

A shy, solemn, vegetarian fella –

Who swipes at bananas,
           gribbity!
                    grabbity!

(They float about in the weak moon gravity.)

In the Sea of Tranquility penguins play,

But the walrus likes to snooze all day,

Till the Zookeeper comes –

eight full pails

Swing from her hands

which have bright green scales.

She's got Neptune salad, Pluto pie,

Stardust sugar from Orion's sky,

Angel fish, meteor bars,

Purple pumpkin from the planet Mars.

Polar bears come floating like big white clouds

Down from their mountain. They're each allowed

A starfish and chips with tomato sauce.

(And a healthy portion of salad, of course!)

Open wide!

The black-and-gold moon tiger leaps and paws,

Scratches a shooting star with his claws.

The Keeper throws him a Jupiter kebab,
(Which a cheeky baby monkey tries to grab!)

The elephants bounce on the silvery dust,

Leaving pockmark footprints on the moon's thin crust.

Their trunks are telescopes

           probing

               space,

Pointing up at the Earth's blue face.

Hippos wallow in the moon's deep craters,

Bobbing with the rhinos and the alligators.

Giraffes stoop low on their space-rocket necks,

And eat their Venus leaves with

delicate

pecks.

The eyes of the panda widen, stare,

At the universe and the bright stars there,

At black holes, planets, distant suns.

Her baby munches on a moon-rock bun.

The moon lion sleeps in his deep dark cave –

But the little Zookeeper's very brave.

She tickles him awake with her eight green hands,

Then spoon-feeds him with whatever he demands!

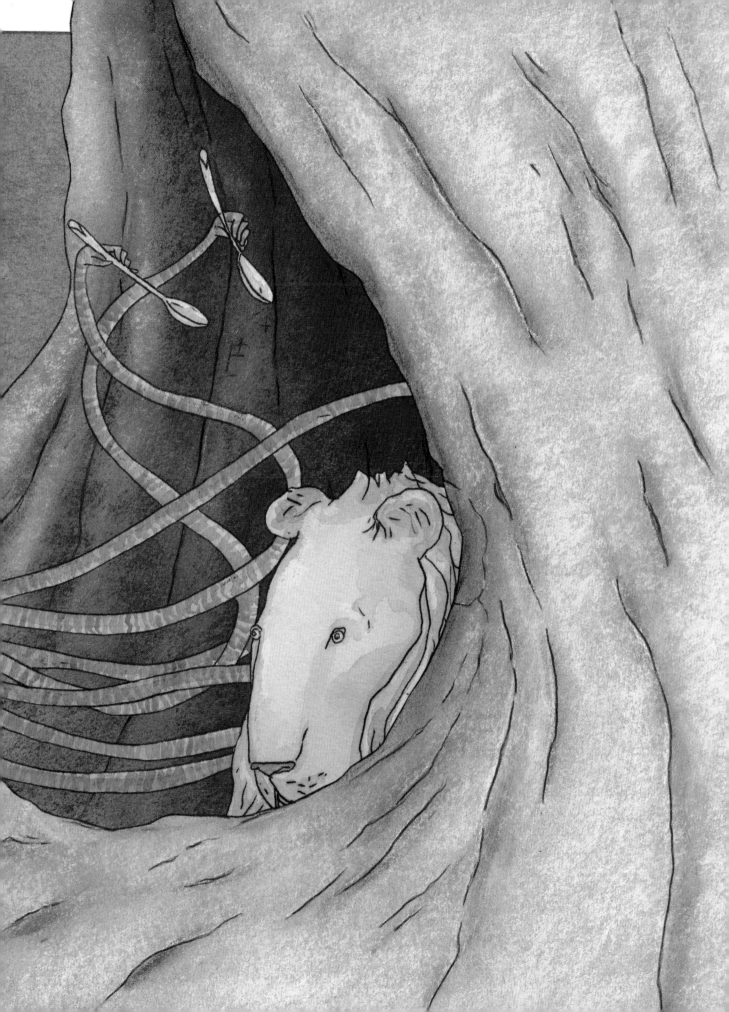

The moon's a plate on the table of the sky,

Licked completely clean. And we all know why!

The Moon Zoo creatures have had their dinner.

(Even the lunar snake could be a bit thinner.)

Empty pails clank as the Zookeeper goes home.
She walks along the Milky Way, all alone,

Spaceships and satellites above her head –
While in the zoo on the moon
they're all in bed.

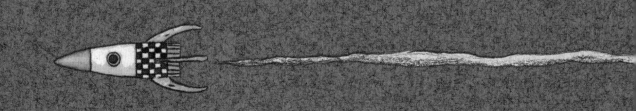